# MUHAMMAD ALI

Published in the United States of America by Cherry Lake Publishing
Ann Arbor, Michigan
www.cherrylakepublishing.com

Reading Adviser: Marla Conn MS, Ed., Literacy specialist, Read-Ability, Inc.

Photo Credits: ©picture-alliance/dpa/Newscom, cover; ©picture-alliance/dpa/Newscom, 1; ©picture-alliance/dpa/Newscom, 5; ©picture-alliance/dpa/Newscom, 6; ©Unknown/Wikimedia, 9; ©Everett Collection/Newscom, 11; ©Bob Gomel/Wikimedia, 12; ©Polaris/Newscom/Newscom, 15; ©The Palm Beach Post via ZUMA Wire/Newscom, 16; ©The Palm Beach Post via ZUMA Wire/Newscom, 17; ©Mark Wilson/Getty Images, 21; ©Scott Olson/Getty Images, 22; ©Thomas Kelley/Shutterstock, 25; ©Will Powers/Getty Images, 26; ©Allan Tannenbaum/Polaris/Newscom, 28; ©Retrographic/mediadrumworld.com via ZUMA Press/Newscom, 28; ©Charles Bertram/Lexington Herald-Leader/TNS/Newscom, 29; ©Allan Tannenbaum/Polaris/Newscom, 29; ©picture-alliance/dpa/Newscom, 30

Library of Congress Cataloging-in-Publication Data has been filed and is available at catalog.loc.gov

Cherry Lake Publishing would like to acknowledge the work of The Partnership for 21st Century Learning.
Please visit *www.p21.org* for more information.

Printed in the United States of America
Corporate Graphics

## ABOUT THE AUTHOR

J.E. Skinner received a Bachelor of Arts in Anthropology from Wake Forest University. She loves writing both fiction and nonfiction books. In addition to reading as much as she can, when J.E. isn't writing, she is hiking with her dogs and spending time with her family in the beautiful outdoors.

# TABLE OF CONTENTS

# Boxing and the Greatest

**B**oxing is one of the oldest sports in the world. The sport has existed since 1500 BCE and has been part of the modern Olympic games since 1904. Fans enjoy the energy and excitement of watching a fight. Viewers watch with anticipation as their favorite fighter walks down the ramp and enters the ring. The fighter throws some jabs and hooks in the air, practicing the punches he'll use against his opponent. The audience at boxing matches feels the intensity that comes from each fighter. If boxers lose their focus for even one second, they can get hit or even knocked out.

To prepare for a fight, **welterweight** champion Floyd Mayweather took part in a 10-week training camp. Mayweather went to the gym five days a week. He **sparred**

Ali trained both in the gym and by running three to five miles (4.8 to 8 kilometers) nearly every day to stay sharp and fit.

with numerous boxers. Boxers train hard because they test their physical and mental limits each time they box. Fans enjoy watching these athletes show their strength and their skill. They admire the risks boxers take, and they appreciate how hard boxers train. Supporters watch their favorite fighters and feel pride in their athleticism and dedication.

Boxing uses the 10-Point Must System to score a fight. A fighter wins the match if he knocks out his opponent. If by the end of the twelve rounds both fighters still stand, the fight is said to have "gone the distance." If this happens, three judges decide

Ali celebrates during a match after knocking his opponent to the mat.

the winner. Judges award a point for hard, clean punches. Boxers must also show good defense. Fighters lose at least one point each time they are knocked down. They also lose a point if they **foul** the other fighter.

Fighters can win a match three ways. Unanimous decision means that all three judges gave the most points to the same fighter. With split decision, two judges declare a winner, and the third judge claims the opponent won. A majority decision occurs when two judges declare a winner, while a third calls a draw. If all

# The Anchor Punch

Aside from Ali's legendary quick footwork, he perfected the Anchor Punch. Fans at the match called it the "phantom punch" because Ali threw it so quickly hardly anyone actually saw it. On May 25, 1965, Ali fought Sonny Liston to defend his **heavyweight** championship. As Liston threw a punch, Ali planted his foot firmly on the ground, and punched over Liston's outstretched arm. His overhand strike landed squarely against Liston's jaw. The force of the blow raised Liston's left foot off the canvas and dumped him in a heap by the ropes. It took Liston two tries to get up. The referee restarted the fight. Within six seconds, Ali had punched Liston several more times, and the referee ended the fight.

the judges say the fighters fought equally well, the fight is ruled a draw.

One of the most well-known fighters was Cassius Clay. He fought 61 **bouts** and won 56 of them. Of those, 37 were knockouts. He won his first 19 fights, 15 of which were knockouts! In 1964, he changed his name to Muhammad Ali. Despite his different names, most people knew him simply as "The Greatest." Unlike other heavyweight boxers, Ali was quick, and he threw hard punches. Ali was good enough to hit hard and move fast—a rare ability for a boxer.

## Fight of the Century

One of the most famous fights of all time took place between Muhammad Ali and Joe Frazier in 1971. It was called The Fight of the Century. It was one of only five fights Ali ever lost. The Fight went a full fifteen rounds. One of Ali's most famous quotes was about this fight. When asked how quickly he moved and how hard he hit, Ali replied, "I float like a butterfly, sting like a bee."

During the 1960 Olympics in Rome, Ali defeated
Pietrzykowski to win gold. Ali was only 18.

# Fast Fists and Political Proclamations

**A**fter only six years as a boxer, Clay was still an amateur when he entered the 1960 Rome Olympics at age eighteen. He won all four of his fights, and became the Olympic light heavyweight champion. Boxing fans took note of Clay's quick and powerful jabs, which delighted onlookers and intimidated opponents. Clay won his first professional bout on October 29, 1960, to police officer Tunney Hunsaker just one month after his Olympic win. Clay opened up a cut over Hunsaker's eye, which swelled shut. Clay easily won the fight. Hunsaker praised Clay, saying "He's awfully good for an 18-year-old and as fast as a **middleweight**." Ali was undefeated for the next 18 fights, until the end of 1963. Of those wins, 15 were by knockout. Fans marveled at Ali's speed and nimbleness, and his impressive knockout record.

Ali speaks with sports journalist Howard Cosell in 1965 to promote an upcoming fight.

Along with boxing, Ali was in the news because he spoke against slavery and how poorly African Americans were treated in the United States. In 1961, Ali joined the Nation of Islam, an African American **Muslim** group. The Nation of Islam, or NOI, said that violence might be necessary to bring about equality both socially and in the workplace. The group spoke openly about the evils of slavery. They thought that African Americans should fight against **racism** in the United States. The NOI encouraged African Americans to fight for equality. Ali became friends with

Malcolm X and Ali celebrate after Ali defeats Sonny Liston
to become the heavyweight world champion.

Martin Luther King Jr. and Malcolm X, two pioneers of the **Civil Rights** Movement. King and Malcolm X disagreed with how to win black freedom. King wanted peaceful protests. Malcolm X was part of the Nation of Islam and supported violence if necessary. Clay supported Malcolm X.

On February 25, 1964, Clay sought to dethrone Sonny Liston as heavyweight champion. Clay arrogantly claimed that Liston was "too ugly to be world champion. The world champ should be pretty like me!" Liston couldn't handle Clay's speed and hard punches. One of his eyes was swollen shut. Liston also sprained his shoulder in the fight. Liston refused to fight in the seventh round due to his shoulder and swollen eye. Clay became the heavyweight champion. This win continued Clay's undefeated streak. Ali proved himself with each fight that he was one of the best boxers who ever lived. The day after he defeated Liston, Clay announced that he had changed his name to Muhammad Ali.

## A Strained Friendship

*Malcolm X chose to leave the Nation of Islam in 1964 because he no longer believed in the group's ideas. Since Malcolm X and Ali were friends, Malcolm X fully expected Ali to leave with him. Ali chose to stay. As a result, he became more popular within the group. His friendship with Malcolm X was broken. In later years, Ali wished they could have stayed friends, and said losing the friendship was his biggest regret.*

# The Coward and the Hero

Ali stayed in the news throughout most of the 1960s. Of his 29 straight wins from 1960 to 1967, Ali knocked out 23 of those opponents. African Americans cheered his bravery both in and out of the ring. He fought against tough opponents, and won every bout. Politically, African Americans were grateful to have such an influential person addressing slavery and **segregation**. Younger white Americans favored Ali as well, both for his athletic **prowess** and for their belief that segregation should end.

Both white Americans and African Americans found an unlikely champion in Ali when he refused to fight in the Vietnam War. The Vietnam War began on November 1, 1955,

In 1966, Ali declared he would not fight in Vietnam because he did not believe in killing another person.

and ended on April 30, 1975. Americans joined the war to fight **communist** North Vietnam from invading South Vietnam. By 1967, American support for the war was heavily divided. Some Americans wanted to keep fighting. Others, mostly minorities and young white Americans, fought the **draft** and called for an end to the battle.

On April 28, 1967, Ali showed up for the draft, but refused to step forward when his name was called. Ali said fighting went against the teachings of the Qu'ran, the Muslim holy book. Ali

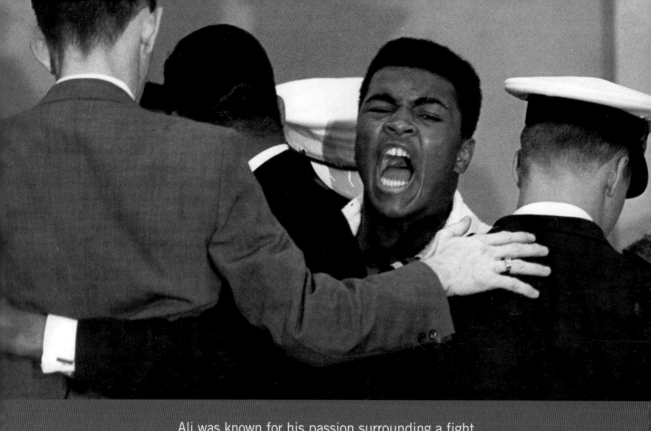

Ali was known for his passion surrounding a fight.

worried that African Americans would get hurt if they went to war. Ali didn't want African Americans to see him sign up to fight, because they might feel obligated to fight, too. He also thought Americans needed to focus on racism in the United States first. Then they could focus on world affairs.

Although many Americans respected his choice, there were several groups of people who called him a coward for not fighting for his country. Ali was immediately arrested. He was banned from boxing in the United States for three years. Ali had to pay a $10,000 fine to the state of New York. In today's

Ali was sentenced to prison for draft evasion and was not allowed to box for 3 years.

money, that would be almost $75,000! He was ordered to go to prison for five years, but he **appealed** the decision. Ali never ended up going to prison. However, the New York State Athletic Commission suspended his boxing license for three years. The World Boxing Association stripped him of his heavyweight **titles**. Ali lost millions of dollars for fights he would have fought if he hadn't been suspended from boxing. Experts think those years would have been his most successful fighting years. Since he couldn't fight, another boxer named Joe Frazier became the heavyweight champion.

## The Medal of Freedom

*On November 9, 2005, former president George W. Bush presented 63-year-old Ali with the Medal of Freedom, the highest civilian award in the United States. President Bush had supported the Vietnam War, while Ali fervently opposed it. Still, Bush commented, "The real mystery, I guess, is how he stayed so pretty. It probably had to do with his beautiful soul." Almost forty years after refusing to fight in the Vietnam War, Ali united Americans in a moment of peace.*

# History Repeats

In August 2016, Colin Kaepernick, the San Francisco 49ers quarterback, refused to stand for the national anthem. It wasn't until his third time sitting that anyone took notice. Kaepernick kneeled for the national anthem to bring awareness to the police brutality and racism occurring throughout the country. His actions bear a striking resemblance to Muhammad Ali's protest of the Vietnam War and his support of the Civil Rights Movement. They were seen as troublemakers ungrateful with their success. The athletes both faced punishment for their decision. Kaepernick was benched for several games. He was also criticized in the media for disrespecting his country, much like Ali when he refused to fight in the Vietnam War.

# Giving Americans Hope

In the late 1970s and into the 80s, Ali's behavior and movements changed significantly. From a swift-footed powerhouse, Ali's gait became slow and shuffling. He trembled and shook. Ali's speech slurred and he had trouble talking. Unable to fight, Ali retired from boxing in 1981. It wasn't until 3 years later, at the age of 42, that Ali was diagnosed with Parkinson's disease. The diagnosis hit him as hard as the punches he used to throw. Like a true champion, Ali met the hardship straight on, refusing to back down. Instead of hiding from his disease, Ali once again put himself in the public eye. He drew attention to Parkinson's and called for research into the disease.

In 1998, Ali teamed up with Michael J. Fox, a well-known actor diagnosed with Parkinson's at 29 years of age. In 2002, they

Actor Michael J. Fox and Muhammad Ali goof around during a
Senate meeting with Health and Human Services.

testified before Congress to raise awareness and fund research for
the disease. The Muhammad Ali Parkinson's Center was set up in
Ali's honor to help those with Parkinson's. A patient of the Center
said of Ali, "He's such a fighter—not just in the ring but in his life.
It's an inspiration to us all."

Ali also spent considerable time working with
**underdeveloped** countries. In 1998, he traveled to Cuba with the
Disarm Education Fund. The Fund uses donations and celebrity
volunteers to encourage governments to focus on the rights and
needs of their citizens. Ali worked with the Disarm Education

Ali met with His Holiness the Dalai Lama in 2003.

Fund to deliver $1.2 million worth of food and medicine to the Cuban people. The Cuban president, Fidel Castro, called Ali's visit a "great **moral** gesture." Ali saw the visit as an opportunity to protest the American **embargo** of Cuban goods.

Muhammad Ali received an audience with Pope John Paul II at the Vatican in 1982. He met with the Dalai Lama in 2003 to dedicate the "Field of Compassion" **interfaith** temple in Bloomington, Indiana. Although a **devout** Muslim, Ali wanted these leaders to talk openly about their experiences and cultures.

He hoped the discussion would lead to a greater understanding and tolerance of other cultures and beliefs.

In 1990, Ali used his fame to negotiate and return fifteen hostages trapped in Iraq. Many Americans were not sure that Ali would succeed. They feared those people would get hurt. However, Ali did amazing work and saved every hostage. Many Americans were proud that he used his fame to protect his fellow Americans.

## Messenger of Peace

Messengers of Peace are people from different fields such as art, literature, music, and sports, who promote goodwill between nations. These volunteers donate their time and talent to raise awareness for the United Nations. They work with the United Nations to bring goodwill and peace to foreign nations. They work to make sure citizens are safe and healthy. Ali was named a Messenger of Peace in 2002 for his work bringing attention to starving citizens in Afghanistan.

# The Greatest

**M**uhammad Ali had six beliefs he thought were important. They were: confidence, conviction, dedication, giving, respect, and spirituality. Confidence means that a person believes in themselves and knows that they are good at what they do. Conviction is a belief that a person feels very strongly about. Dedication is a strong support for someone or something. Giving means that a person shares what they have because they like to be kind and help others. Respect means that a person accepts other people's ideas and feelings. Spirituality has to do with what people believe about their souls or their spirit. Muhammad Ali had very strong feelings about these beliefs. He wanted to teach others about them. He thought it could help people treat each other and themselves better. Ali believed that people should have strong

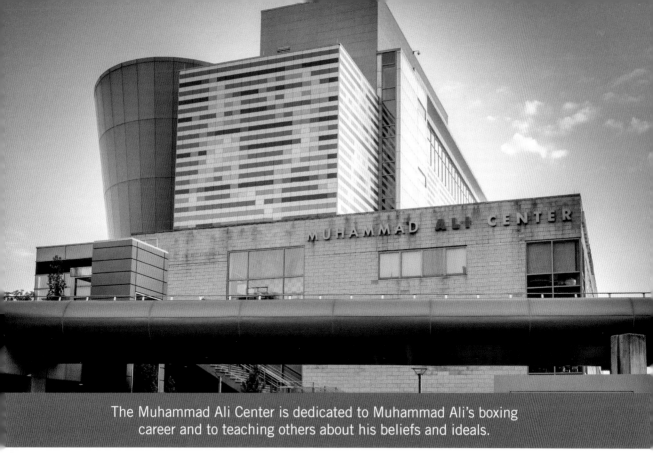

The Muhammad Ali Center is dedicated to Muhammad Ali's boxing career and to teaching others about his beliefs and ideals.

beliefs, but also respect other people's beliefs. He set up the Muhammad Ali Center to teach people how to use these beliefs to inspire others.

The Center holds many programs designed to enrich the lives of those living in the community. One such program is the Daughters of Greatness. The Ali Center periodically promotes women who talk about the impact they have made in different communities. These women range in their careers from social work, to acting, to business and investing. The women speaking

Muhammad Ali and his wife, Lonnie, in 2006.

at these events seek to encourage, inspire, and change the way
women think about themselves, and how they interact with the
world.

Another program from the Center was inspired by an event
from Ali's childhood. When his red bike was stolen, Ali reported
to a policeman that he would "whup" whoever stole it. The officer,
Joe Martin, told Ali he needed to learn how to fight before he
could whup anyone. He trained Ali for the next six years. Ali
pursued a career in boxing. He used his status as a celebrity to
bring awareness to racism in the United States. Although Ali

started as a fighter, he became a pacifist and toured the world, bringing a message of peace and unity. The Red Bike Moment Program helps youth identify a moment in their lives when they felt strong and empowered to make a change in their lives. Youth can share stories with each other and inspire others in the community to find their own Red Bike Moment. Communities can use these moments to empower themselves and serve the needs of their citizens.

## The G.O.A.T.

*This was one of Ali's nicknames, and it stood for Greatest of all Time. Ali proved he was the Greatest many times, both in his athletic and public life. He was a three-time heavyweight champion. He helped countries and people in need. Ali always fought for African American rights, no matter what it cost. He made many choices that certain people disagreed with. Still, Ali never changed his beliefs because other people told him to.*

**1961**

Joins the Nation of Islam.

**1967**

Refuses to be drafted into the Army. He is stripped of his boxing title and is forbidden from boxing.

**1960**

Wins gold at Rome Olympics, and wins his professional fight against Tunney Hunsaker.

**1940**

**1960**

**1970**

**1942**

Born Cassius Marcellus Clay in Louisville, KY.

**1970**

Returns to the ring and defeats Jerry Quarry.

**1964**

Defeats Sonny Liston to become the world heavyweight champion and changes his name to Muhammad Ali.

**1990**
Negotiated the release of 14 hostages with Iraq's leader, Saddam Hussein.

**2016**
Ali dies due to complications of a respiratory illness.

**1984**
Diagnosed with Parkinson's disease.

1980

1990

2010

**1981**
Loses his last boxing match to Trevor Berbick.

**1998**
Traveled to Cuba and donated $1.2 million worth of food and medicine to the people there. Kofi Annan names Ali a Messenger of Peace.

**1996**
Lights the Olympic cauldron at the Summer Olympic Games in Atlanta.

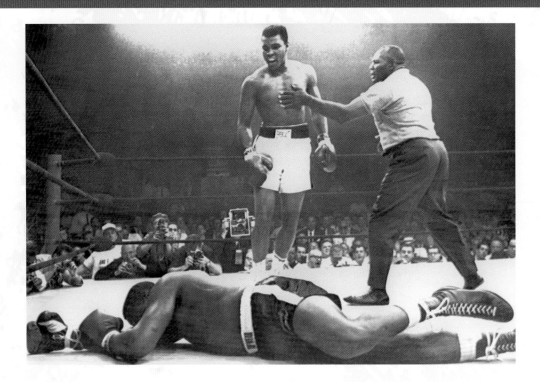

In this photo, Ali knocked Liston out using a new technique called the Anchor Punch. What does Ali creating a new boxing technique say about his importance to the sport?

Look at Ali's posture and body language. What kind of emotions and feelings do you think Ali instilled in his opponents? Were they afraid of him?

In the mid-1960s, when this photo was taken, the United States was experiencing the Civil Rights Movement and the Vietnam War. How did Ali's confidence and boldness inspire and give hope to the American people?

# Learn More

## BOOKS

Buckley, James Jr. *Who Was Muhammad Ali?* New York: Penguin Workshop, 2017.

Garrett, Leslie. *The Story of Muhammad Ali.* New York: DK Publishing, 2002.

Myers, Walter Dean. *The Greatest: Muhammad Ali.* New York: Scholastic Press, 2001.

## ON THE WEB

**The Ali Center**
https://www.alicenter.org

**History**
http://www.history.com/topics/black-history/muhammad-ali

**Muhammad Ali**
http://muhammadali.com

# GLOSSARY

**appeal (uh-PEEL)** to apply to a higher court for reversal of a decision of a lower court

**bouts (BOUTS)** boxing matches or fights

**civil rights (SIH-vul RAITS)** the rights of citizens to political and social freedom and equality

**communist (KOM-yoo-nist)** a person who follows the system of social organization based on the holding of all property in common, with ownership of goods ascribed to the community as a whole or to the state

**devout (dih-VOUT)** devoted, pious, religious

**draft (DRAFT)** the enforcement of the government requiring all able-bodied persons to join a country's military

**embargo (em-BAHR-go)** any restriction on commerce by order of the government

**foul (FOUL)** to strike an opponent unfairly or illegally

**heavyweight (HEH-vee-wayt)** a weight class in professional boxing for boxers weighing 175 pounds (79.4 kilograms) and over

**interfaith (IN-tur-fayth)** having to do with various people following different religions

**middleweight (MIH-dul-wayt)** a weight class in boxing ranging from 160 to 174 pounds (72.6 to 78.9 kg)

**moral (MOR-uhl)** relating to the principles of right and wrong

**Muslim (MUHZ-lim)** a follower of the religion of Islam

**prowess (PROW-is)** skill or expertise in a particular activity or field

**racism (REY-sih-zum)** prejudice, discrimination, or antagonism directed against someone of a different race, based on the belief that one's own race is superior

**segregation (seh-grih-GAY-shun)** the enforced separation of different racial groups in a country, community, or establishment

**spar (SPAHR)** to box lightly for practice

**titles (TAI-tulz)** championships

**underdeveloped (un-dur-dih-VEH-lupt)** something that is less developed; when talking about countries, underdeveloped means poorer and with fewer resources in education, health care, and industry

**welterweight (WEHL-tur-wayt)** a weight class in boxing ranging from 147 to 159 pounds (66.7 to 72.1 kg)

# INDEX